JACK and the BEANSTALK

Adapted and illustrated
by
Tony Ross

Delacorte Press/New York

Published by
Dell Publishing Co., Inc.
1 Dag Hammarskjold Plaza
New York, New York 10017

This work was first published in Great Britain in 1980 by
Andersen Press Ltd.

Printed in Great Britain
First U.S.A. printing

Library of Congress Cataloging in Publication Data

Jack and the beanstalk.
  Jack and the beanstalk.
  SUMMARY: A boy climbs to the top of a giant
beanstalk where he uses his quick wits to outsmart
a giant and make a fortune for himself, his mother,
and his sister.
  [1. Fairy tales. 2. Folklore—England.
3. Giants—Fiction] I. Ross, Tony.
PZ8.J15Ro   398.2'1'0941 [E]   80-67493

ISBN 0-440-04168-6
ISBN 0-440-04174-0 (lib. bdg.)

JACK and the BEANSTALK

Jack Trotter lived with his mother, his sister, Polly, and his cat, Bodger, on an old, run-down farm. The farm had once been prosperous, but that was when Jack's father had been around to look after things. The story was that Jack's father had been cheated out of all his money and had left town with a broken heart.

So Jack, his mother, and Polly—and sometimes the cat— tried to run the farm, but without much success. They were happy though, and had lots of fun together. They kept chickens, geese, and sheep, but their proudest possession was a fine cow.

Not only did the cow give milk, she also helped with the work. She pulled the plow and dug up potatoes with her horns.

Life was good on the Trotter farm until...

...the bad weather came. The deep snow killed off all the crops and the geese and the hens. The Trotters became poorer than ever, with only last year's moldy old potatoes to eat.

One spring morning Jack's mother was down to the last moldy potato.

"You'll have to go to market and sell the cow," she told her son. "Then we can buy some food." No one wanted to sell the cow, but it had to be done.

On the way Jack met a smart fellow in a tall hat and new clothes.

"I could use a nice cow like that," he said to Jack. "I'll swap it for my magic bean."

"Thank you, sir!" said Jack, taking the bean.

Jack rushed home in great excitement. "Look, Mother," he cried. "I exchanged our cow for a bean!"

Jack's mother turned white, then purple, then red. She was *furious*. "A BEAN!" she screeched. "You swapped our cow for a BEAN!" In her temper she threw an old can at Jack. Jack tried in vain to explain that it was a *magic* bean, but his mother was in no mood to talk to him.

Polly giggled as empty cans bounced off her brother's head.

By this time even Jack wasn't too sure if his bean was magic, but he planted it just in case. That night, while the Trotters were asleep, a beanstalk grew, and grew, and grew, and GREW, and...

...GREW. By morning the beanstalk stretched way beyond the clouds. Before anyone else was up, Jack stood staring at his magic plant. "Must see what's at the top of that!" he gasped.

It was a hard climb. At the top of the beanstalk Jack stepped out into a strange land. In the distance he spotted a little old lady who was busy gathering mushrooms. "Hello," he called to her. "Could you offer me a bite to eat?"

The old lady was friendly but seemed a little nervous as she led Jack to a tall, somber house. While they were struggling up the steps, a terrible voice rattled over the trees: "FEE FIE FO FUM... I SMELL THE BLOOD OF A LITTLE ONE!"

"The GIANT!" squeaked the old lady in fright. She pushed Jack through the massive front door. "Quick, hide in the oven. It's not lit!"

As Jack scrambled into the oven the giant clumped into the house.

He was enormously tall, hideously ugly, and had bad breath. Jack peeked at him through a crack.

"Housekeeper," the giant boomed to the old lady. "I can smell a little one! Cook him and bring him for my dinner!"

"There's *no* little one, sir," answered the old lady. "You can have a nice bit of pork though!"

"Oh, very well," grumbled the giant, sitting down at the table.

The giant gobbled down his pork and fifty-six pounds of potatoes.

"Bring me my wonderful hen," he snorted at the end of his meal. "I want some more golden eggs."

So the old lady brought the hen.

The giant soon fell asleep, counting the eggs. Jack watched
in wonder from the oven. I'll have that hen, he thought.
Climbing onto the table, he grabbed the hen, and bolted
out of the giant's house.

Jack reached the beanstalk and leaped onto it. The angry giant, awakened by the hen's cackles, was not far behind him, firing his cannon wildly.

But luckily he did not notice the beanstalk.

The hen laid golden eggs every day, and the Trotters soon became rich.

With less work to do Jack became bored and decided to climb the beanstalk again to see what else he could get.

Once again Jack hid in the oven. After an enormous dinner of rhinoceros and garlic, the giant called for his golden pieces.

He eventually fell asleep counting the gold, and Jack crept up and swept it all into a sock.

Jack struggled down the beanstalk. It was hard work, as giants' socks are large, and gold is heavy. Mother, Polly, and Bodger were there to meet him, worried by his second trip to the giant's land.

However, when they saw the gold pieces, all was forgiven. They whooped and leaped about, tossing gold into the air and singing songs about being richer than ever. Then they went to the shops and bought the finest clothes they could find, and an expensive dog.

With a hen who laid golden eggs and a sock full of gold pieces, the Trotters were rich enough to live in comfort to the end of their lives.

Now that they were so rich, the Trotters went out walking in the best part of town. They enjoyed it when other rich people bowed low and said "How d'ye do!" to them.

But Jack soon became bored with having everything and craved adventure once more.

Although everybody begged him not to go, he was away up the beanstalk again.

It was dark when he reached the top.

The old lady was there to meet him, and they could hear the
giant returning home for his dinner. "Quickly," gasped the old
woman. "Into the oven with you."

"FEE FIE FO FUM...I SMELL THE BLOOD OF A LITTLE
ONE," roared the giant as he came up the stairs.

Quickly the old lady plonked a plate of steaming whale in front of the giant. When he had eaten it, the giant called for his wonderful singing harp. Inside the oven Jack listened to the exquisite voice of the magic harp. That one thing would make my life happy! he thought. At last the giant fell asleep.

Jack snatched the harp and dashed to the beanstalk. Instead of singing, the harp cried out, "HELP, MASTER, I'M BEING STOLEN! HELP! HELP! HELP!"

This time the giant followed Jack to the beanstalk and began to climb down.

Scrambling to the ground, Jack ran and snatched his ax.
  The giant was still above the clouds as Jack hacked at the
beanstalk. There was a wobble and a snap and the giant
crashed down to earth.

The Trotters lived happily ever after. They spent many happy evenings listening to the harp (as these were the days before television). They even made a swimming pool out of the hole made by the giant's crash.

And what of the giant?

Well, some say he fell so fast, he went right down through the earth and came out on the other side. Others say he lives in the middle of Australia, with no one to pester but the kangaroos (who don't like him at all). The old lady still lives in the huge house in the sky. She has no hard work to do and she eats chocolates all day.

Really, Jack stole nothing at all. Do you remember that Jack's father lost all his money many years ago? The poor, witless fellow was tricked out of his wealth by the giant, so Jack only took back what was rightfully his...but that's another story.

About the Artist

Tony Ross is a popular illustrator who has
been widely acclaimed for his versions of familiar
folktales. He lives in Cheshire, England, and teaches art
at the Manchester Polytechnic School.

About the Book

The art for *Jack and the Beanstalk* was prepared in
ink and watercolor. The book was printed by Cowell's
of Ipswich, England.